ARCTIC OCEAN

EUROPE

ASIA

*Yenisey-Angara River*

Lake Baikal
Siberia

Krasnohorska stalagmite
Slovakia

*Volga River*

GOBI
DESERT

Mount Vesuvius
Italy

Mount Elbrus
Georgia

*Caspian Sea*

Mount Fuji
Japan

Mount Etna
Sicily

K2
China

Mount Everest
China/Nepal

*Chiang Jiang River*

*Marianas Trench*

ARABIAN
DESERT

*Ganges River*

Shillong Plateau
Meghalaya State
India

SAHARA DESERT

Khône Falls
Laos

Mount Tambora
Sumbawa
Indonesia

Lake Chad
Chad

AFRICA

*Nile River*

Cave Chamber
Sarawak

Lake Victoria
Kenya/Tanzania/Uganda

INDIAN
OCEAN

Mount Wilhelm
Papua New Guinea

Boyoma Falls
Zaire

Mount Kilimanjaro
Tanzania

Lake Tanganyika
Rwanda/Tanzania/Zaire/Zambia

Lake Malawi
Malawi/Mozambique/Tanzania

Mount Krakatoa
Sunda Strait
Indonesia

AUSTRALASIA

*Great Barrier Reef*

Victoria Falls
Zambia/Zimbabwe

AUSTRALIA

KALAHARI
DESERT

AUSTRALIAN DESERT

*Murray Darling River*

N
NW    NE
W            E
SW    SE
S

ANTARCTICA

# HIGHEST
# LONGEST
# DEEPEST

## A Fold-out Guide to the World's Record Breakers

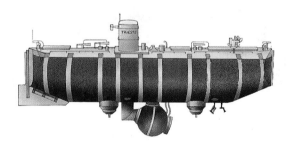

**Written by John Malam**
**Illustrated by Gary Hincks**

**Simon & Schuster Books for Young Readers**

SIMON & SCHUSTER BOOKS FOR YOUNG READERS
An imprint of Simon & Schuster Children's Publishing Division
1230 Avenue of the Americas, New York, New York 10020

J
910
M

SIMON & SCHUSTER BOOKS FOR YOUNG READERS
is a trademark of Simon & Schuster.

This book was conceived, edited, and designed by
Marshall Editions
170 Piccadilly, London W1V 9DD

First American Edition, 1996

10 9 8 7 6 5 4 3 2 1

Library of Congress Catalog Card Number: 96-69517

ISBN: 0-689-80951-4

**Editor:** Claire Berridge
**Designer:** Ian Winton
**Managing Editor:** Kate Phelps
**Art Director:** Branka Surla
**Editorial Director:** Cynthia O'Brien
**Picture Research:** Zilda Tandy
**Production:** Janice Storr, Selby Sinton

Originated in Italy by Ad Ver, Bergamo
Printed and bound in Italy by Officine Grafiche de Agostini, Novara

The publishers would like to thank Andrew Farmer for illustrating
the following pages: Planet Earth, pp. 8–9; Weather Extremes,
pp. 38–39; and the endpaper world map.

**Picture credits**
*tl*=top left; *tr*=top right; *bl*=bottom left; *br*=bottom right; *mr*=middle
right; *ml*=middle left

10 G. Hinterleitner/Frank Spooner Pictures; 12 Royal Geographical
Society; 15 John Cleare/Mountain Camera; 17 Richard Kirby/Oxford
Scientific Films; 19*tr* John Shaw/Bruce Coleman; 19*tl* Zefa Pictures;
24*ml* Peter Carmichael/Aspect Picture Library; 24*mr* Robert Harding
Picture Library; 24*bl* Zefa Pictures; 24*br* Martin Wendler/NHPA;
26 Randy Wells/Tony Stone Images; 28 Prof. Stewart Lowther/Science
Photo Library; 29 Piers Cavendish/Impact; 30 Robert Harding Picture
Library; 37 Chris Sharp/South American Pictures

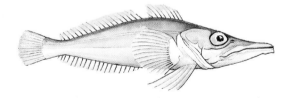

# CONTENTS

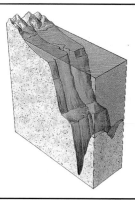

# PLANET EARTH

The nine planets in our solar system travel around the sun

**E**arth is one of nine planets known in our solar system. Seen from space, our world seems tiny. It is just one of countless millions of stars, planets, and moons. But Earth has a special position in the universe, for it is the only place where life is known to exist.

Our planet has grown up over millions of years. The continents have drifted into their present-day positions, seas have filled the hollows, animal species have died out, and some newcomers, such as humans, have appeared on this extraordinary planet.

Arctic Ocean

North Pole •

The Arctic Ocean is the smallest ocean

▼ *A slice through time*
*Great changes have occurred during the 4,600 million years of Earth's history. Shown here is how the Earth's land mass divided into continents and how life evolved before the first humans emerged on the planet.*

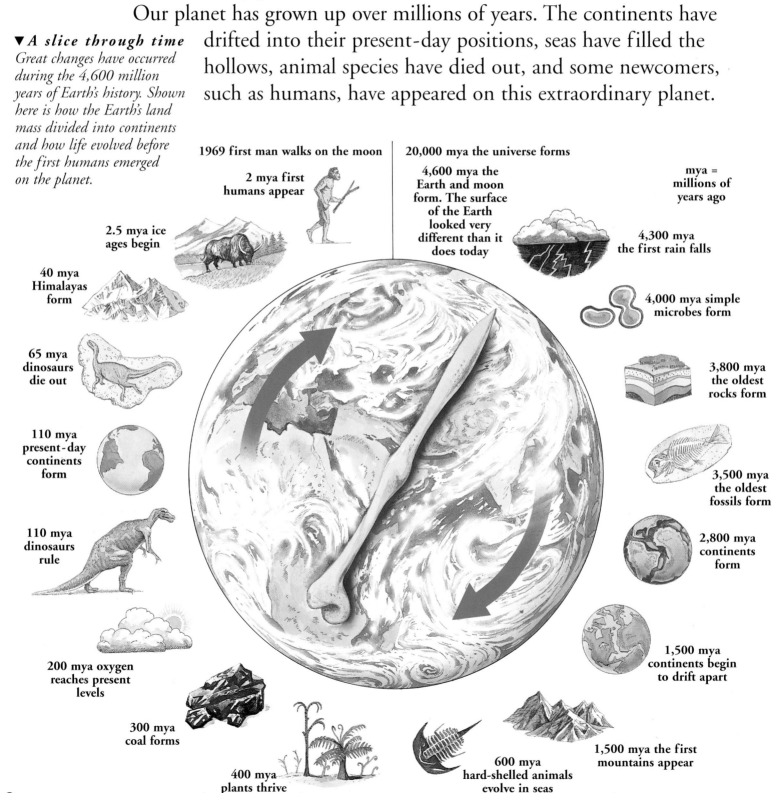

1969 first man walks on the moon

2 mya first humans appear

2.5 mya ice ages begin

40 mya Himalayas form

65 mya dinosaurs die out

110 mya present-day continents form

110 mya dinosaurs rule

200 mya oxygen reaches present levels

300 mya coal forms

400 mya plants thrive

600 mya hard-shelled animals evolve in seas

1,500 mya the first mountains appear

1,500 mya continents begin to drift apart

2,800 mya continents form

3,500 mya the oldest fossils form

3,800 mya the oldest rocks form

4,000 mya simple microbes form

4,300 mya the first rain falls

mya = millions of years ago

20,000 mya the universe forms

4,600 mya the Earth and moon form. The surface of the Earth looked very different than it does today

8

Europe
Africa
Atlantic Ocean

**Africa is the warmest of the continents**

North America
South America

**North America is the third biggest continent**

Pacific Ocean

**The Pacific Ocean is the biggest ocean**

Asia
Indian Ocean   Australasia

**Asia is the biggest continent**

Antarctica
South Pole •

**Antarctica is the coldest place on Earth**

▲ *Land and sea*
*The Earth's surface is two-thirds water and one-third land. The land is made up of seven continents; the water includes four oceans and many seas, lakes, and rivers.*

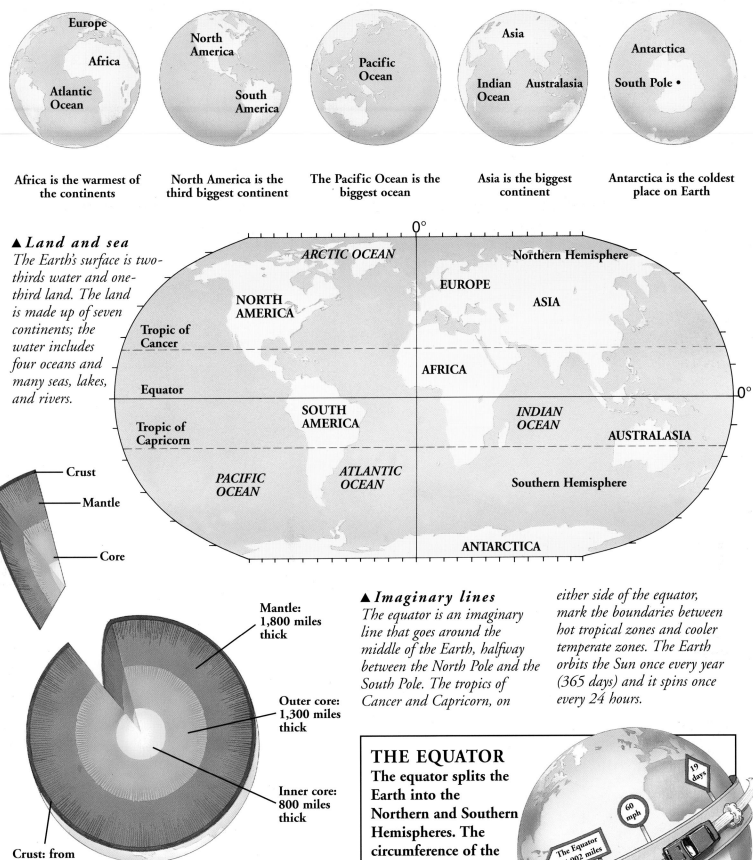

0°

ARCTIC OCEAN

Northern Hemisphere

EUROPE

ASIA

NORTH AMERICA

Tropic of Cancer

AFRICA

Equator

0°

SOUTH AMERICA

INDIAN OCEAN

Tropic of Capricorn

AUSTRALASIA

PACIFIC OCEAN

ATLANTIC OCEAN

Southern Hemisphere

ANTARCTICA

Crust

Mantle

Core

Mantle: 1,800 miles thick

Outer core: 1,300 miles thick

Inner core: 800 miles thick

Crust: from 3 to 30 miles thick

▲ *What's it made of?*
*The Earth was made when gravity pulled clouds of dust and rock together. This made heat, which melted dust and rock, forming the core, mantle, and crust.*

▲ *Imaginary lines*
*The equator is an imaginary line that goes around the middle of the Earth, halfway between the North Pole and the South Pole. The tropics of Cancer and Capricorn, on* *either side of the equator, mark the boundaries between hot tropical zones and cooler temperate zones. The Earth orbits the Sun once every year (365 days) and it spins once every 24 hours.*

## THE EQUATOR
**The equator splits the Earth into the Northern and Southern Hemispheres. The circumference of the equator is 24,902 miles. Traveling in a car at 60 miles per hour, it would take 19 days to drive around the equator.**

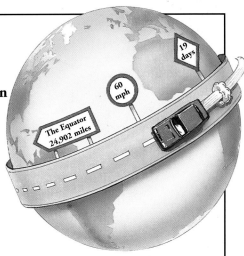

19 days

60 mph

The Equator 24,902 miles

# HIGHEST MOUNTAINS

**M**ountains are found on the surface of the world and even under the sea.

*Climbing is a demanding, exhilarating, popular sport*

They can be solitary high points or linked in ranges that run for hundreds of miles. The Alps in Europe, the Andes in South America, and the Himalayas in Asia are mountain ranges, each with peaks that rise for thousands of feet.

The Earth's surface is restless and is constantly cracking open and causing the continents to drift. Mountains rise up where the surface is under pressure. As long as there is pressure, mountains keep their appearance—but when the pressure stops they start to wear away. Over millions of years, even the tallest mountains will turn to rubble.

## ▼ "Iceman" of the Alps
*In 1991, German tourists found the well-preserved body of a man 12,000 feet up in the Alps, near the border of Italy and Austria. Trapped in ice, the "Iceman" was 5,300 years old. He may have died when he was caught in a snowstorm as he was crossing the mountains.*

Elbrus, Georgia, Europe
18,510 feet

Mont Blanc, France, Europe
15,771 feet

## HOW ARE MOUNTAINS MADE?
The Earth's surface (or crust) is made of giant sections called plates. They are always drifting. Where plate edges touch, the land buckles and is folded over, rising up to make mountain ranges such as the Himalayas.

**Plate movement**

**BEFORE**

Earth's crust

Plate movement

Folded sediment

**AFTER**

## ▶ Mountain people
*Sherpas live in Sikkim and Nepal in the foothills of the Himalayas. They believe the mountains are home to their gods. They are famous as mountain traders and guides.*

Mount McKinley,
Alaska, North America
20,320 feet

Mount Kilimanjaro,
Tanzania, Africa
19,340 feet

Mount Wilhelm,
Papua New Guinea,
Australia
14,793 feet

▼ *Highest living
mammal*
*Sure-footed yaks can
climb as high as 20,000
feet in the Himalayas. The
Tibetans use them to carry
heavy packages (or bundles),
and as sources of milk, meat,
leather, and cloth.*

## AFRICAN GIANT
The giant groundsel, with its
head of spiky leaves, grows
20 feet high on Africa's
Mount Kilimanjaro.

Long-haired
male yaks

11

**CONQUERING EVEREST**
In 1953, Edmund Hillary (from New Zealand) and Tenzing Norgay (a Sherpa from Nepal) became the first to climb Everest.

Mauna Kea, Hawaii, Pacific Ocean 32,000 feet

**▼ Even taller than Everest**
*At 32,000 feet, the dormant volcano of Mauna Kea in Hawaii is just taller than Mount Everest—but 18,000 feet of it lies under the Pacific Ocean.*

Mount Everest, China/Nepal, Asia 29,028 feet

K2 (Mount Godwin-Austen), China/Pakistan, Asia 28,250 feet

**▶ K2—a strange name?**
*The world's second highest peak is in the Karakoram range of mountains. As it was the second mountain in this range to be surveyed, it was named "K2."*

Aconcagua, Argentina, South America 22,834 feet

**▼ High flier**
*Soaring for hours on its large wings, the Andean condor can withstand the fierce mountain winds.*

**▲ The highest peaks**
*Nine of the world's highest mountains are in the Himalayas, formed as the Earth's crust crumpled and was pushed upward.*

Mount McKinley, Alaska,
North America
20,320 feet

**▶ Mountain life**
*Padded hooves help the chamois
and ibex to climb over jagged
rocks. The marmot hibernates
until it is warm enough
in the mountains to
wake up.*

Mount Wilhelm,
Papua New Guinea,
Australia
14,793 feet

Mount Kilimanjaro,
Tanzania, Africa
19,340 feet

**◀ Mountain guides**
*Sherpas help and guide
mountaineers on expeditions in
the Himalayas. They are known
for their endurance of harsh
mountain conditions.*

Chamois

Alpine
marmot

Ibex

## HOW OLD ARE MOUNTAINS?

The shape of a mountain tells you
if it is young or old. The Rocky
Mountains, in North America, are
young, made approximately 100
million years ago. They are jagged with
rough sides. The Appalachians, also in
North America, are old, made about
250 million years ago. The weather
has worn them down and made
them more rounded.

Jagged young
mountains

Rounded old
mountains

13

# LONGEST GLACIER

The ice fish lives near the seabed in Antarctic waters

**A** glacier is a mass of ice built up from snow that has fallen over tens of thousands of years. When snow falls on mountains faster than it melts, it stacks up in layers. As the snow presses down, the lower layers turn to ice, and a glacier is formed. A glacier is moved slowly downhill by gravity, changing the shape of the land beneath it as it pushes forward. When a glacier melts, it leaves behind a valley littered with rocks and other material brought down in the ice.

Glaciers are found in mountain ranges on every continent except Australia. They store about 75 percent of the world's freshwater. The world's longest glacier is the Lambert Glacier, which flows for 440 miles across Antarctica. About 90 percent of the world's glacier ice is in the frozen continent of Antarctica.

## THE BIGGEST ICE SHEET
Antarctica, the world's fifth largest continent, is completely covered by ice. The ice sheet is big enough to cover the United States and much of Canada. It is up to two miles thick. If it melted, the world's sea level would rise by more than 200 feet.

WEDDELL SEA

Lambert Glacier

South Pole •

ANTARCTICA

Vinson Massif 16,864 feet

The end of a glacier is called its snout

## PERIL OF THE SEA
When glaciers reach the sea, lumps of ice break off and float away. These are icebergs. In 1912, the *Titanic* struck an iceberg in the Atlantic and sank. Over 1,500 people drowned.

Nine-tenths of an iceberg is below the waterline

A cirque is a bowl-shaped hollow where the glacier starts

Head of the glacier

Another glacier comes in from the side

▲ **Glacial valley**
*A glacier carves a valley in the surface of the Earth as it moves slowly along.*

A glacier flows slowly downhill, carving out a new valley as it goes

As the glacier moves, it scrapes away what lies in its path

## ANTARCTIC WILDLIFE
Penguins live on the floating pack ice; shrimplike krill, fish, squid, octopuses, seals, and whales swim in the cold water; and seabirds such as albatrosses and petrels fly in the windy skies.

Emperor penguin and its young

The leopard seal is one of four seal species found in Antarctica

◀ **The albatross**
*The wandering albatross soars over Antarctic seas. Its wing span is up to 10 feet across.*

▶ **Weather in an ice tube**
*Scientists have visited Antarctica since the early 1900s. By drilling out tubes of ice, they learn about past changes in the continent's climate.*

15

# DEEPEST LAKE

**Skating on Lake Baikal during the winter's great freeze**

A lake is a still body of water that is surrounded by land. Most lakes contain freshwater, but some (such as the Dead Sea in Israel and Jordan) hold salt water. Lakes are formed in natural hollows which have been made by movements of the Earth, and which then become traps for water.

The deepest lake in the world is Lake Baikal in Siberia, Russia. It has another claim to fame—it is also the world's oldest freshwater lake, formed between 20 million and 30 million years ago, when earth movements caused the ground to open up, making a rift of over one mile deep. More than 300 rivers drain into the lake. It is thought that Lake Baikal holds about 20 percent of all the freshwater in the world.

### ▼ Types of lakes
*Crater lakes form in the craters of extinct volcanoes. Glacial lakes form in ice-scoured hollows. Oxbow lakes are the remains of old river channels.*

**Crater lake**

**Glacial lake**

**Oxbow lake**

### ▼ Lake Baikal's valuable catch
*The sturgeon, a much-prized fish, lives in Lake Baikal. It is almost scaleless and has a long snout and toothless mouth. Sturgeons are famous for their blackish roe (eggs). When salted the eggs become "caviar."*

### ◄ Life underwater
*Many different animals live in Lake Baikal's cold waters. Scientists who have searched the lake's depths looking for animal life believe it holds more than 1,500 species. Some animals such as the unusual golomyanka fish, which is completely transparent, are found only in Lake Baikal and nowhere else in the world. Shrimp and freshwater sponges have been spotted living at the very bottom of the lake—more than a mile below the surface.*

**Sediment at the bottom of the lake**

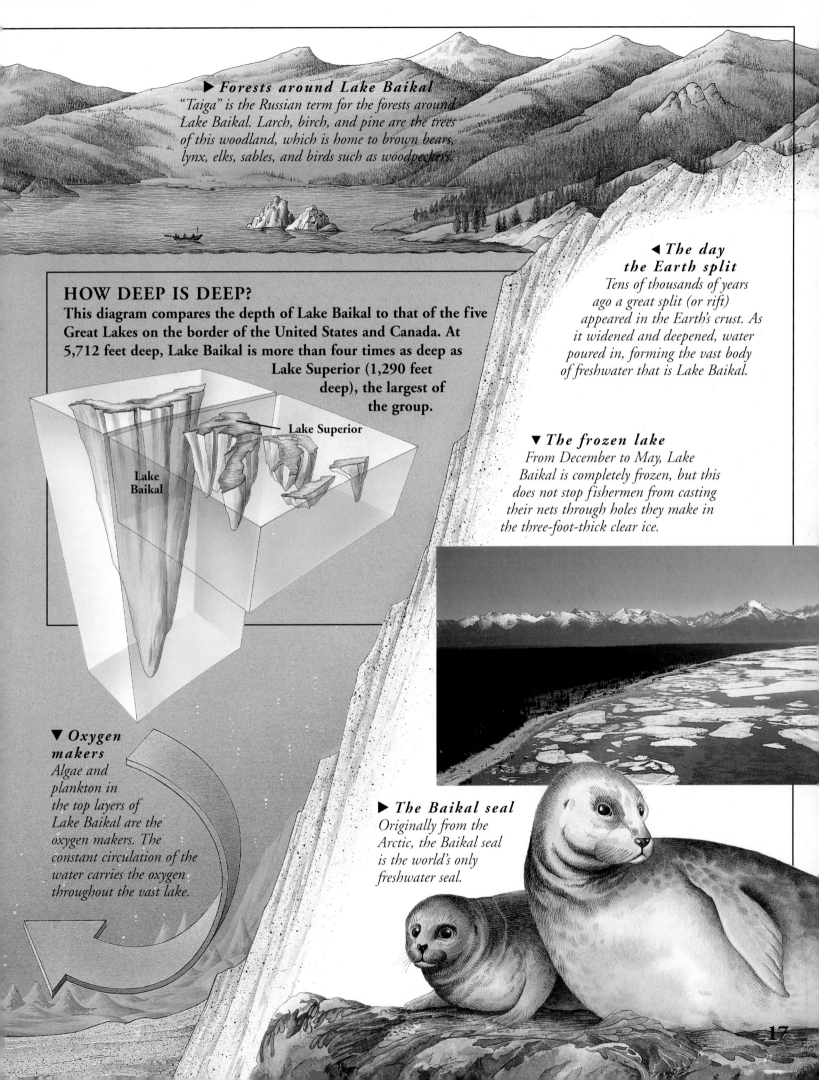

### ▶ Forests around Lake Baikal

"Taiga" is the Russian term for the forests around Lake Baikal. Larch, birch, and pine are the trees of this woodland, which is home to brown bears, lynx, elks, sables, and birds such as woodpeckers.

## HOW DEEP IS DEEP?

**This diagram compares the depth of Lake Baikal to that of the five Great Lakes on the border of the United States and Canada. At 5,712 feet deep, Lake Baikal is more than four times as deep as Lake Superior (1,290 feet deep), the largest of the group.**

Lake Superior

Lake Baikal

### ◀ The day the Earth split

Tens of thousands of years ago a great split (or rift) appeared in the Earth's crust. As it widened and deepened, water poured in, forming the vast body of freshwater that is Lake Baikal.

### ▼ The frozen lake

From December to May, Lake Baikal is completely frozen, but this does not stop fishermen from casting their nets through holes they make in the three-foot-thick clear ice.

### ▼ Oxygen makers

Algae and plankton in the top layers of Lake Baikal are the oxygen makers. The constant circulation of the water carries the oxygen throughout the vast lake.

### ▶ The Baikal seal

Originally from the Arctic, the Baikal seal is the world's only freshwater seal.

17

# BIGGEST DESERT

The desert rose is actually a rock found in deserts

Every continent has deserts, from the sandy "seas" of Africa to the icy wastes of Antarctica. The world's biggest hot desert is the Sahara in North Africa. It is about the size of the United States.

The Sahara has not always been the dry desert we know today. Until about 5,000 years ago, the climate there was milder and wetter. Many plants, animals, and people lived in the region. But then the climate changed. Less rain fell, plants died, and the animals and people moved away. The wind blew the soil cover off and weathered the bedrock into sand, which it heaped up into vast areas of dunes.

But despite the changed scenery, life adapted, and the Sahara now supports plants and animals that have learned how to survive there.

Vultures

▼ *A sea of golden sand*
*For as far as the eye can see, the sand dunes of the Sahara rise and fall like waves. The wind shapes them. Sand blows up their gentle slopes, then rolls down the steep slopes.*

Desert rock formations

Antelope

▲*A desert of rock and stone*
*Where does desert sand come from? It comes from the rock that forms the desert floor. As the rock is worn away by wind and extremes of heat and cold, rock columns and "pavements" of stone are left. In time, the rock is worn into grains of sand — which the wind heaps up into the dunes of sand deserts.*

Fennec fox

Scorpion

Desert spider

Beetle

18

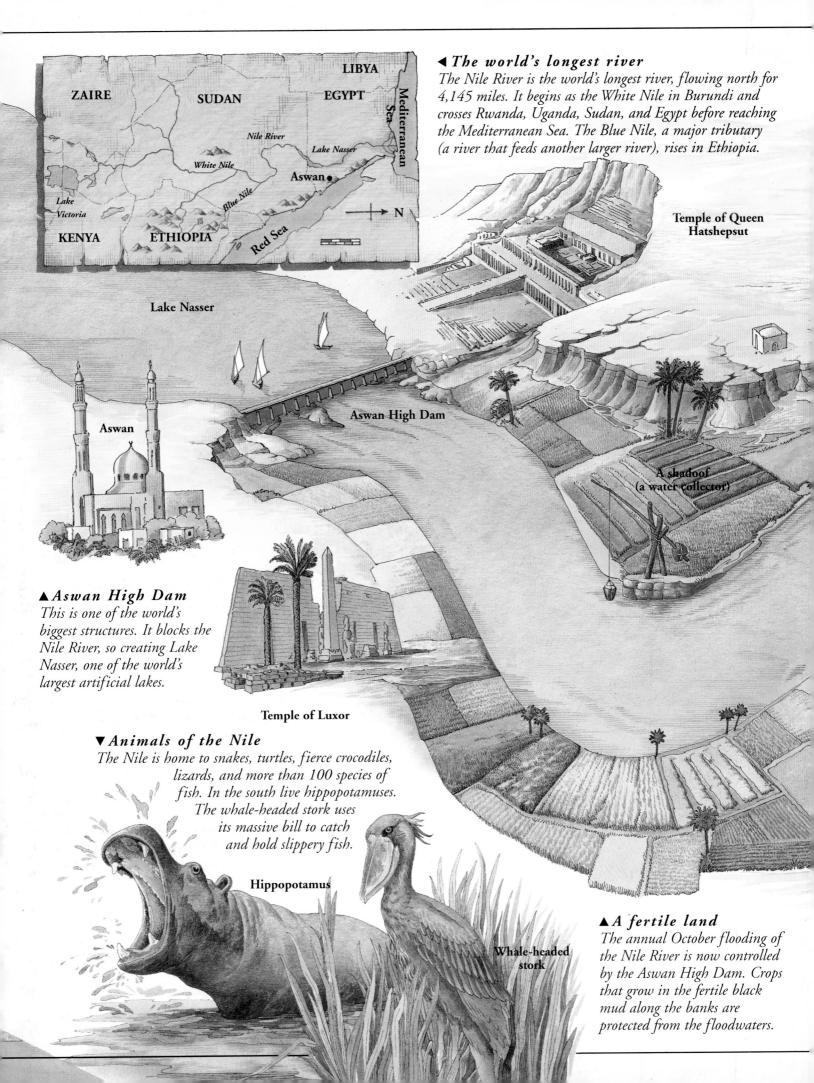

**ZAIRE** **SUDAN** **LIBYA** **EGYPT**

*Nile River*

*Lake Nasser*

*White Nile*

Aswan●

*Lake Victoria*

*Blue Nile*

**KENYA** **ETHIOPIA**

*Red Sea*

**N**

Mediterranean Sea

### ◄ *The world's longest river*
The Nile River is the world's longest river, flowing north for 4,145 miles. It begins as the White Nile in Burundi and crosses Rwanda, Uganda, Sudan, and Egypt before reaching the Mediterranean Sea. The Blue Nile, a major tributary (a river that feeds another larger river), rises in Ethiopia.

**Temple of Queen Hatshepsut**

**Lake Nasser**

**Aswan High Dam**

**Aswan**

**A shadoof (a water collector)**

### ▲ *Aswan High Dam*
This is one of the world's biggest structures. It blocks the Nile River, so creating Lake Nasser, one of the world's largest artificial lakes.

**Temple of Luxor**

### ▼ *Animals of the Nile*
The Nile is home to snakes, turtles, fierce crocodiles, lizards, and more than 100 species of fish. In the south live hippopotamuses. The whale-headed stork uses its massive bill to catch and hold slippery fish.

**Hippopotamus**

**Whale-headed stork**

### ▲ *A fertile land*
The annual October flooding of the Nile River is now controlled by the Aswan High Dam. Crops that grow in the fertile black mud along the banks are protected from the floodwaters.

### ▼ Australian desert

Australia has the world's second largest desert. Parts of the sandy desert are "live," changing shape as the wind blows. Other parts are "dead," where vegetation has taken hold and stopped the dunes from moving. Uluru (Ayers Rock, below) rises above the desert plain.

### ▲ Prickly water towers

The Sonoran Desert in Arizona is the main desert of the North American continent. Here the fingerlike saguaro cactus soaks up rainwater and stores it in its trunk and branches. The largest of these desert water towers can hold as much as one ton of water — enough to last it until the next time it rains.

### ▼ Ships of the desert

Camels are the workhorses of the Sahara, able to withstand the intense heat, carry heavy loads, and go without water for several days.

Camels

### ▶ Desert dwellers

Tuaregs live in the Sahara near oases. They are nomads, moving from one campsite to the next. They often wear veils to protect their faces from the sun, wind, and sand.

Snake

Tuareg people

### ◀ Desert animals

Many animals have learned how to survive in the desert. They keep cool in the shade, can go for a long time without water, and can move easily over sand or burrow into it.

Jerboa

Rain

Evaporation

Underground flow

# WHERE DOES AN OASIS GET ITS WATER FROM?

An oasis needs a constant supply of water, which it attracts from miles around. As rain falls it seeps into the ground and is stored in porous (water-bearing) rock. An oasis forms where a natural hollow dips into the underground water supply.

Date palm tree

### ▼ *Life at the water hole*

*An oasis is the desert's own "filling station," a place at which all roads cross and thirsty travelers stop. Camels drink gallons of water to build up their energy for the journey ahead. Date palms provide shade and tasty, energy-rich fruit.*

Oasis

Locust

# LONGEST RIVERS

A softshell turtle found in the Nile

**R**ivers are the highways of the **natural world.** Over thousands of years they change the face of the land, carving out long, deep valleys and spreading fertile sediment across their wide floodplains and deltas. Plants and animals find that rivers are good places to live, and people depend on them for drinking water, for transportation, and as providers of hydroelectric power. Rivers bring much-needed water to farmers.

When Egypt's Lake Nasser was created in the 1960s, this temple at Abu Simbel was moved to dry land above the waterline

They also help drain away excess floodwater from surrounding land. Many of the world's towns and cities, both ancient and modern, are built on the banks of mighty rivers—a sure sign of how much people need these arteries of life.

The continents of Africa and South America are home to the world's two longest rivers—the Nile and the Amazon. Until the building of a major dam, the Nile's yearly flood washed fertile mud downstream. The ancient Egyptians were so dependent on the mud for farming that they even named their land after it—Kemet, the "land of the black mud." On the other side of the world, the mighty Amazon feeds vast rainforests and supports the lives of countless plants and animals which grow and live along its banks.

Glacier

Waterfall

Gorge

Oxbow lake

Floodplain

Delta

Ocean

## HOW A RIVER IS FORMED

One way a river begins is as water running off from a mountain glacier. As the glacier slowly releases its water, it flows downhill by the quickest route. The trickle of meltwater is soon joined by water that has fallen as rain. This stream follows gulleys, pours over sheer drops as waterfalls, and carves out steep-sided gorges in its race to level ground. And when it finds flat ground, its pace slows as it meanders across its wide floodplain, before finally making its way to the sea.

◄ *Coral barrier*
*An aerial view of the barrier reef and lagoon off the volcanic island of Bora-Bora, South Pacific.*

▼ *Life on the reef*
*More than 5,000 different species of animals and plants live on the reef itself. Colorful fish, fanlike corals, delicate anemones, and sponges are just some of the reef's inhabitants.*

Vasiform sponge

Feather star

**CORAL MAKER**
This is a coral polyp, a tiny creature with a rocky skeleton.
A coral reef is made from billions of their skeletons.

Mouth

Tentacle

Rocky skeleton

Ridge coral

Cup sponges

Sandy sea cucumber

Gorgonian coral

Biscuit sea star

Scorpion fish

Sea urchin

Sea urchin

Brain coral

Hard coral

Daisy coral

Triton

Harlequin tuskfish

Ghost crab

**The Step pyramid, the first pyramid built**

**▲ The desert**
Ninety percent of Egypt's land is empty desert. Nine out of ten people in Egypt live along the Nile River.

**▼ The wonders of ancient Egypt**
For more than 3,000 years the civilization of ancient Egypt flourished along the course of the Nile River. Today, the temples, pyramids, and statues created by the Egyptians remind us of the splendors of their long-lost world.

**Pyramid and Sphinx**

**▼ Nile Delta**
The mouth of the Nile is a fan-shaped delta, formed by thousands of years of silt deposits washed downriver.

**Felucca**

**Tourist cruise boat**

**The mask of Tutankhamun**

**Nile crocodile**

**▶ Cairo**
The capital of Egypt is Cairo, the largest city in Africa with a population of eight million. Iron and steel, cars, textiles, and tourism are its chief industries. The Nile provides the city with drinking water.

**Papyrus reed boat**

## WHICH IS THE MIGHTIEST RIVER?

The Nile might be the longest, but it is the Amazon that wins the title "mightiest river." As its many tributaries feed into it, enough water is poured each day into the Atlantic Ocean to supply water to all the homes in the United States for more than five months. The Nile, in comparison, is 200 times smaller in the volume of water it carries.

Nile, Africa, 4,145 miles

Amazon, South America, 4,000 miles

Chiang Jiang, Asia, 3,964 miles

Mississippi-Missouri, North America, 3,710 miles

Murray-Darling, Australia, 2,330 miles

Volga, Europe, 2,290 miles

### ▼ Chiang Jiang (Yangtze)

*Chiang Jiang, the Chinese name for their longest river, the Yangtze River, means the "great river" or the "long river."*

### ▼ Rhine

*The Rhine is the main river of western Europe. It rises in a Swiss glacier, flows through Europe, and runs into the North Sea.*

### ▼ Mississippi-Missouri River system

*These linked rivers form the longest river system in the United States. Mississippi means "father of waters" in the Algonquian language. Steamboats have used the river since the 1800s.*

**Anaconda**

### ▼ Amazon

*The snakelike Amazon in South America is the world's second longest river. The anaconda snake, which grows to 25 feet, lives in the surrounding forest.*

**Caiman crocodile**

Mangroves

# LONGEST CORAL REEF

White-tipped reef shark

The nautilus is related to the squid and the octopus. It has up to 90 arms with which to grab its prey

**The longest coral reef in the world is the Great Barrier Reef.** It lies in the Coral Sea off the northeast coast of Australia and is actually a series of coral islands and reefs that stretch for more than 1,250 miles. The warm, clear, shallow salt water is the perfect environment for coral and a rich variety of other animals and plants. For hundreds of thousands of years, billions and billions of tiny coral animals (called polyps) have attached themselves to the reef. These living creatures, which look like sea anemones, are brightly colored. When they die they leave their limestone skeletons fixed to the reef. New coral animals soon attach themselves to the skeletons of their ancestors, and so a never-ending cycle of life goes on, as the reef constantly grows and renews itself.

Sweetlips

Stingray

Butterfly fish

Turtle

LAGOON

Wrasse

Staghorn coral

Textile cone

Brittle star

25

# TYPES OF REEF

Atoll

Barrier reef

Fringing reef

A fringing reef is always attached to land, often a volcanic island. It lies just below the surface of the sea. A barrier reef is separated from the shore by a lagoon. The reef makes a barrier between the land and the sea. An atoll is the final stage of a reef where the land sinks under the surface of the sea, leaving a ring of coral.

Barracuda

Lion's mane jellyfish

Jacks

Whale shark

▲ *Life on the reef edge*
*At the edge of the coral reef live animals that can withstand the slightly cooler water and stronger current. Sharks come in close, as do schools of fish and drifting jellyfish.*

Turtle grass

Giant clam

Fairy basslets

Orange-tailed damsel fish

Sea fan

Sea star

## AN APPETITE FOR CORAL

The crown-of-thorns starfish is an enemy of the Great Barrier Reef. It dissolves the reef with stomach juices, then eats the mixture to leave plate-sized patches of dead coral. Scientists are trying to control its spread.

27

# VOLCANOES

**A** volcano is a hole in the Earth from which molten (liquid) rock and gas erupt. There are about 850 active volcanoes in the world, and many more that are dormant (sleeping) or extinct (no longer active). Volcanoes can cause great damage, bury towns under ash and lava, set off tidal waves, and throw dust so high into the atmosphere that it travels right around the globe. But they can be beneficial, too. They can create new land and islands. Their fiery underground heat can be tapped to provide a source of hot water and energy.

Pele, a fierce fire goddess, is believed to live in the crater of a volcano on the island of Hawaii

### THE SLEEPING GIANT AWAKES
On May 18, 1980, Mount St. Helens erupted after having been dormant for 123 years. The explosion was so great that the summit of the mountain was blown off and vegetation and trees for hundreds of miles around were killed.

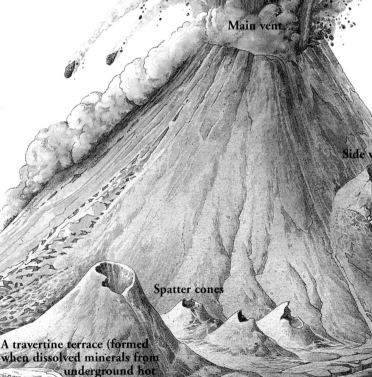

Main vent

Side vent

Spatter cones

A travertine terrace (formed when dissolved minerals from underground hot springs solidify)

Lava flow

Hot mud

# DIFFERENT TYPES OF VOLCANOES

A composite volcano is tall and steep sided. It has frequent lava eruptions. A cinder cone volcano is flatter and throws out gas and ash. A shield volcano has several openings (vents), out of which flows lava. A fissure volcano occurs along a crack in the Earth's crust, letting lava out over a long distance, usually under the sea.

Composite volcano

Cinder cone volcano

Shield volcano

Fissure volcano

**▼ Volcanic landscape**
*Geysers, hot springs, and hot mud pools occur in land heated by the underground activity of volcanoes.*

**◄ Hot water**
*Underground hot springs in Iceland are a source of geothermal power (heat energy from within the Earth). People can also bathe in the hot pools created by these springs.*

Fulmar

Crater lake

Geyser

Hot springs

Secondary volcanic cone

Mayweed

Coconut shoots

Monitor lizard

Butterfly

**► Life after the bang**
*Plants and animals soon colonize the new land. Seeds blow in on the wind, and animals arrive shortly after.*

Snake

Cactus

Scorpion

# CAVES

**The cave swiftlet lives in Asian caves. Its nests of translucent saliva are used to make bird's nest soup**

**C**aves are among the greatest of nature's wonders, and yet many still remain unexplored. Hollowed out of solid rock by the non-stop action of water, the world's caves reveal a stunning array of rock formations, bizarre sightless creatures, and paintings made by cave dwellers from long ago.

Caves can be huge caverns, deep holes, or systems that run for miles. At 348 miles, Mammoth Cave, Kentucky, is the longest cave system in the world, while Réseau Jean Bernard Cave, France, with a depth of 5,036 feet, is the deepest known cave in the world.

## STALACTITES AND STALAGMITES
Stalactites cling tightly to the cave roof while stalagmites grow upward from the floor. These strange formations are made from mineral deposits left after dripping water evaporates.

▶ *Record breaker*
*The longest known stalactite in the world, in Cueva de Nerja, Spain, is 195 feet.*

▼ *Cave dwellers*
*The cold, wet, dark conditions of caves are ideal for some animals, many of whom never see daylight.*

▲ *Mighty shape*
*The tallest known stalagmite is in Krasnohorska, Slovakia, at 105 feet.*

Midges

Centipede

Cave frog

Snail

Slug

Cave spider

▶ **Bats and caves**
Beyond the cave mouth is the twilight zone, a clammy near-black environment where bats roost.

▼ **Giant cave**
At 2,300 feet long, 980 feet wide, and 230 feet high, Sarawak Chamber, Malaysia, is the world's largest single cave chamber.

Stream

Joints in rock

Sink hole

Underground river

Cave

Lake

## WHAT MAKES CAVES?
Most caves develop in limestone. Acidic rainwater seeps into cracks in the stone, dissolving it away. Chambers and passages are formed. As the water drains away, the spaces fill with air and dry out.

▶ **Life in the dark**
In the ever-dark world of cave pools live strange eyeless creatures such as fish and shrimps, as well as crayfish and salamanders.

Blind cave fish

Two kinds of blind shrimp

Crayfish

Cave salamander

▶ **Longest underwater cave**
Nohoch Na Chich, Mexico, has more than 13 miles of underwater caves.

# DEEPEST OCEAN

**O**ceans and seas are the bodies of salt water that cover more than two-thirds of the Earth's surface. The biggest ocean of all is the Pacific Ocean, covering almost one-third of the entire planet. Its surface is dotted with over 25,000 islands, which is more than the total number in the rest of the world's oceans added together. The Pacific is also the world's deepest ocean, with an average depth of more than two miles. At one place the Marianas Trench dives down for seven miles—that's about seven times deeper than the famous Grand Canyon in Arizona, making it the deepest known point on the surface of the Earth. The oceans are still mostly unexplored realms, but as diving technology improves, the secrets of the deep are slowly being revealed.

Pacific Ocean

As dry land gives way to sea, the edge of a continent slopes down ever deeper to the ocean depths

Seaweed

Sea horse

Mussels

Crab

Blue shark

Mackerel

Snake eel

Octopus

Continental shelf

Sponges

Turtle

**▼Life on the slope**
*One of the wonders of the ocean is the continental slope—a long, steep-sided drop that marks the edge of a continent and teems with animal and plant life.*

Continental slope

Lantern fish

Feather star

Squid

Shellfish

# HIGHEST WATERFALL

Some plants grow only in fast-flowing water

**W**aterfalls are wonders of the natural world. Some, such as Angel Falls, the highest waterfall in the world, spill like narrow ribbons down cliffs for thousands of feet. Others, such as Khône Falls, fall in wide curtains across several miles.

All waterfalls are capable of generating great amounts of energy because the force of the water falling over them is extremely powerful. As waterfalls wear away the rock over which they pour, they move back upstream, leaving steep-sided gorges behind them. In this way, Niagara Falls has moved backward 1,000 feet in 300 years.

Gorge

River

Hard rock

Plunge pool

Waterfall cuts into rock to form gorge

Hard rock

Water erosion

Plunge pool

Soft shale

### ▲ *The parts of a waterfall*
*A river flows over a cliff. Where the water hits the ground, a plunge pool is formed. Soft rock behind the pool is scoured out. The waterfall recedes (moves backward), leaving a gorge in the rock.*

### ◄ *Waterfall daredevils*
*People have plunged over Niagara Falls in barrels, while others have crossed the falls on tightropes!*

Salmon

Niagara Falls, United States/Canada, is one of the world's best-known waterfalls

Khône Falls, Laos, Asia, is the world's widest waterfall

Torrent duck

Dipper

### ▶ *Waterfall animals*
*Salmon can swim against the surging current in a river and leap up small waterfalls. The dipper and the torrent duck are both birds that live and feed near waterfalls.*

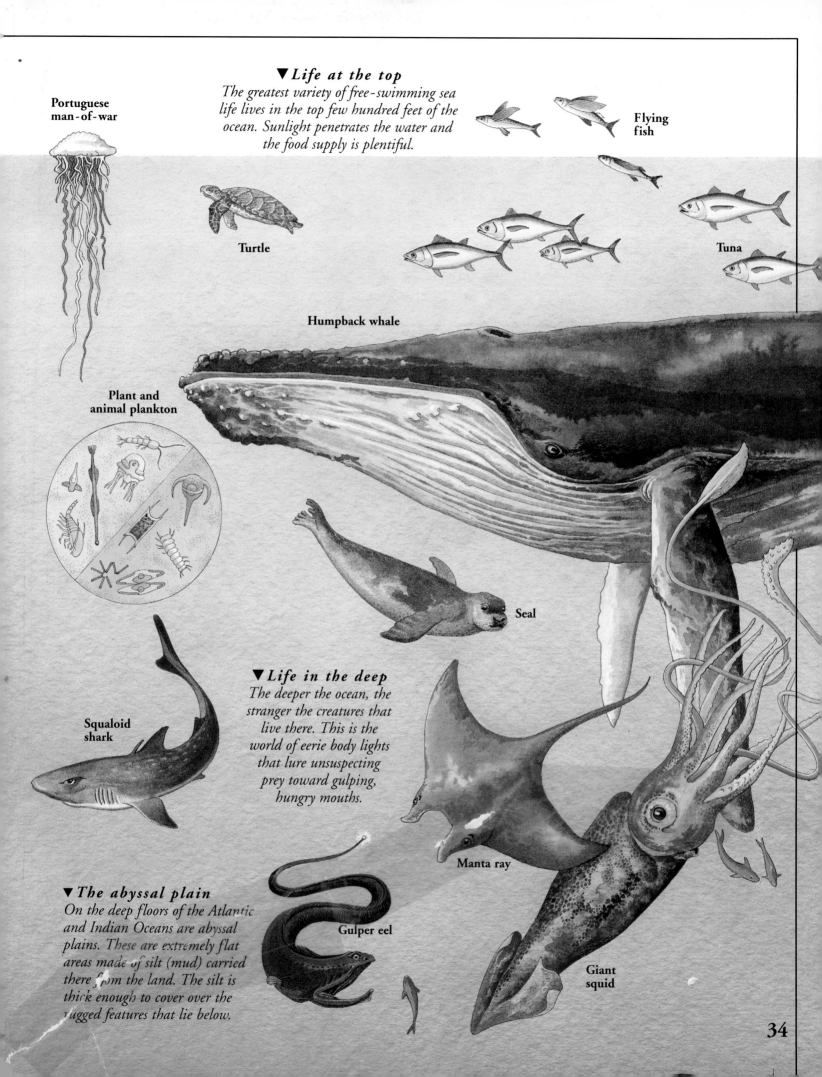

**Portuguese man-of-war**

▼ **Life at the top**
*The greatest variety of free-swimming sea life lives in the top few hundred feet of the ocean. Sunlight penetrates the water and the food supply is plentiful.*

**Flying fish**

**Turtle**

**Tuna**

**Humpback whale**

**Plant and animal plankton**

**Seal**

**Squaloid shark**

▼ **Life in the deep**
*The deeper the ocean, the stranger the creatures that live there. This is the world of eerie body lights that lure unsuspecting prey toward gulping, hungry mouths.*

**Manta ray**

**Giant squid**

▼ **The abyssal plain**
*On the deep floors of the Atlantic and Indian Oceans are abyssal plains. These are extremely flat areas made of silt (mud) carried there from the land. The silt is thick enough to cover over the rugged features that lie below.*

**Gulper eel**

**▲ The Trieste**
This deep-sea bathyscaphe reached new depths in 1953, going down to 10,330 feet. It revolutionized ocean exploration.

**▲ Into the abyss**
The Marianas Trench on the floor of the Pacific Ocean is the deepest known point on the Earth's surface. It has been explored by unmanned robots. It is nearly seven miles deep. A two-pound weight would take one hour to fall to the bottom!

**▲ Restless ocean floor**
The ocean floor is a hostile world of deep-sea trenches, ridges, and volcanoes. The Earth's crust is always renewing itself here with layers of lava. In other places where two pieces of crust touch, one slides under the other to leave a trench.

**▲ Life in the smoke**
In the cold and dark at the bottom of the Pacific Ocean, hot liquids and gases boil up through vents in the Earth's crust, giving rise to "black smokers." Tube worms, shellfish, and some fish live in these pockets of warm water.

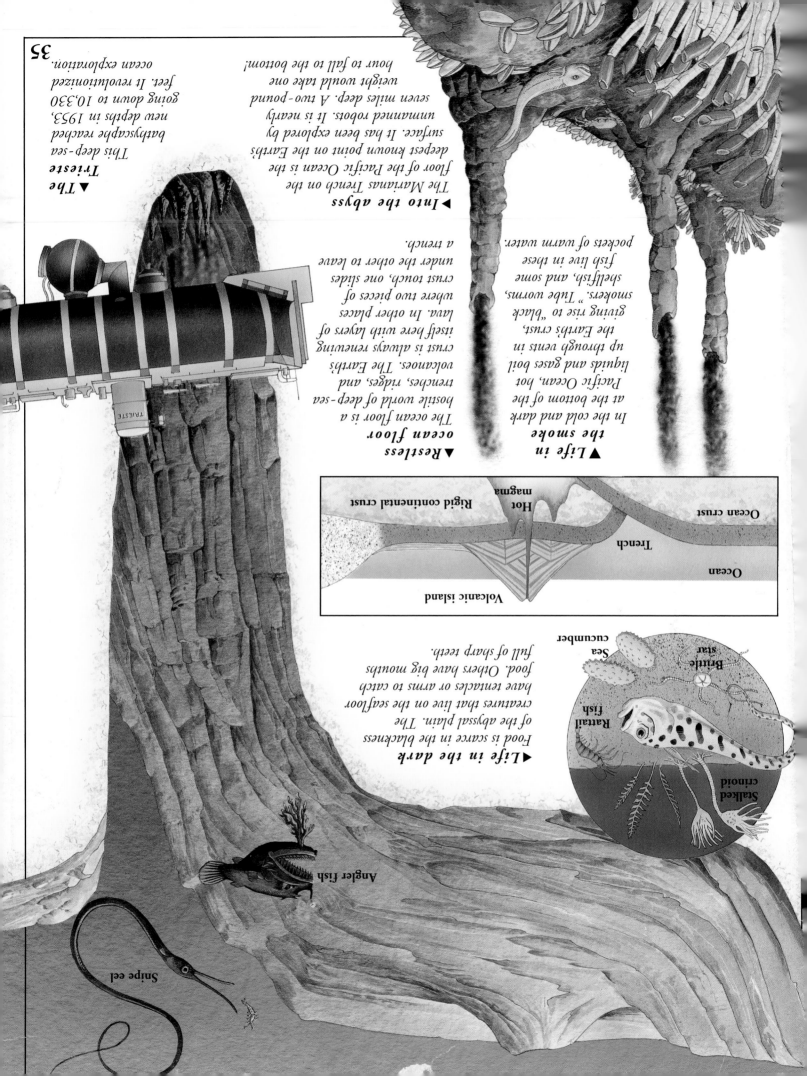

Rigid continental crust

Hot magma

Ocean crust

Trench

Ocean

Volcanic island

**▲ Life in the dark**
Food is scarce in the blackness of the abyssal plain. The creatures that live on the seafloor have tentacles or arms to catch food. Others have big mouths full of sharp teeth.

Sea cucumber

Brittle star

Rattail fish

Stalked crinoid

Angler fish

Snipe eel

TRIESTE

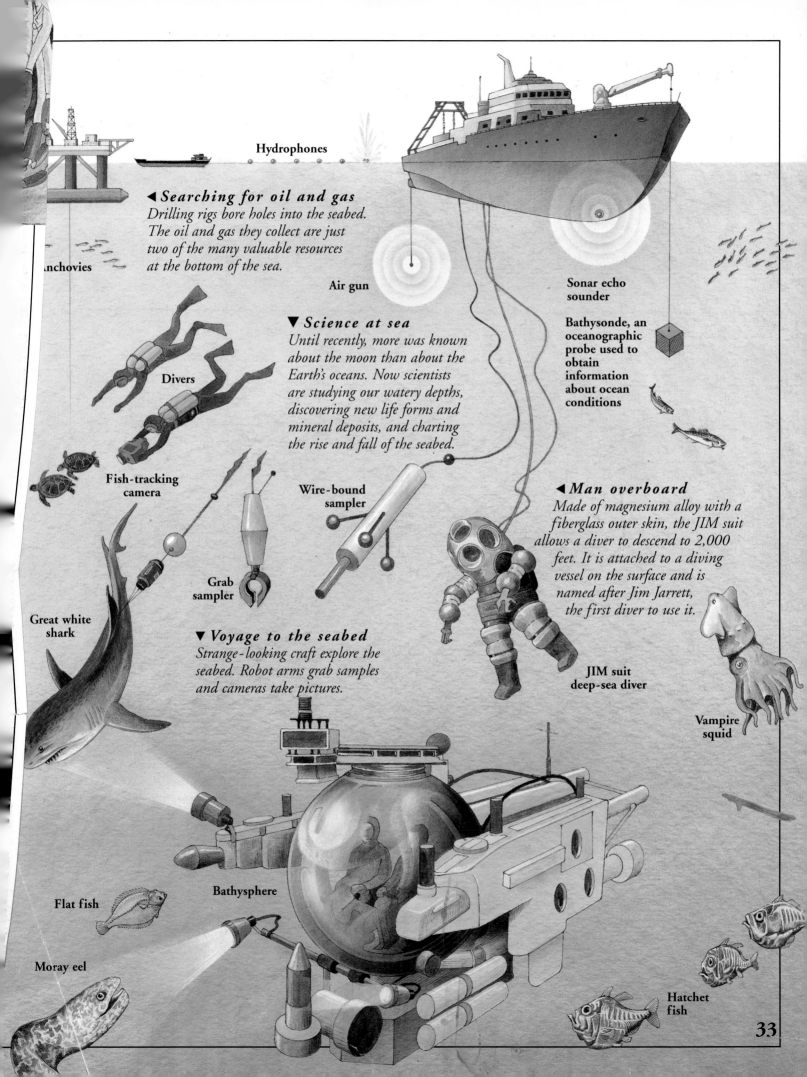

**Hydrophones**

**◄ _Searching for oil and gas_**
Drilling rigs bore holes into the seabed.
The oil and gas they collect are just
two of the many valuable resources
at the bottom of the sea.

**Anchovies**

**Air gun**

**Sonar echo
sounder**

**▼ _Science at sea_**
Until recently, more was known
about the moon than about the
Earth's oceans. Now scientists
are studying our watery depths,
discovering new life forms and
mineral deposits, and charting
the rise and fall of the seabed.

**Bathysonde, an
oceanographic
probe used to
obtain
information
about ocean
conditions**

**Divers**

**Fish-tracking
camera**

**Wire-bound
sampler**

**◄ _Man overboard_**
Made of magnesium alloy with a
fiberglass outer skin, the JIM suit
allows a diver to descend to 2,000
feet. It is attached to a diving
vessel on the surface and is
named after Jim Jarrett,
the first diver to use it.

**Grab
sampler**

**Great white
shark**

**▼ _Voyage to the seabed_**
Strange-looking craft explore the
seabed. Robot arms grab samples
and cameras take pictures.

**JIM suit
deep-sea diver**

**Vampire
squid**

**Flat fish**

**Bathysphere**

**Moray eel**

**Hatchet
fish**

33

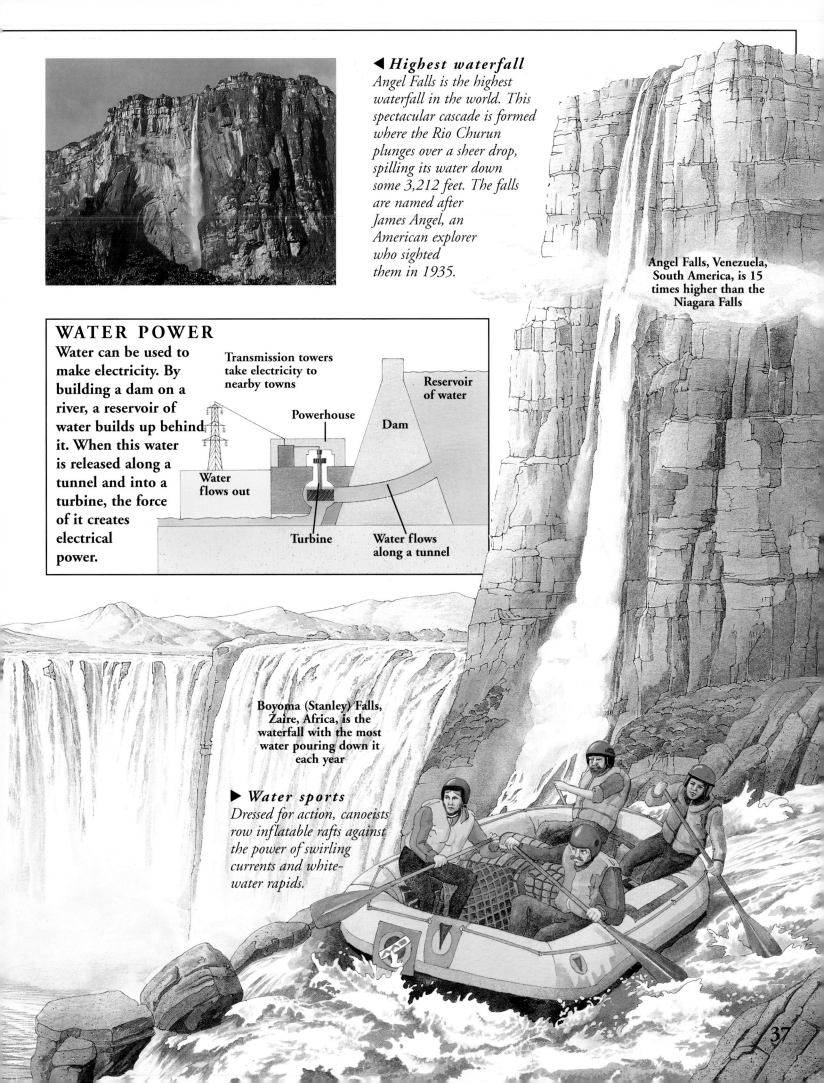

**◄ Highest waterfall**
Angel Falls is the highest waterfall in the world. This spectacular cascade is formed where the Rio Churun plunges over a sheer drop, spilling its water down some 3,212 feet. The falls are named after James Angel, an American explorer who sighted them in 1935.

Angel Falls, Venezuela, South America, is 15 times higher than the Niagara Falls

## WATER POWER

Water can be used to make electricity. By building a dam on a river, a reservoir of water builds up behind it. When this water is released along a tunnel and into a turbine, the force of it creates electrical power.

Transmission towers take electricity to nearby towns

Powerhouse

Reservoir of water

Dam

Water flows out

Turbine

Water flows along a tunnel

Boyoma (Stanley) Falls, Zaire, Africa, is the waterfall with the most water pouring down it each year

**► Water sports**
Dressed for action, canoeists row inflatable rafts against the power of swirling currents and white-water rapids.

# WEATHER EXTREMES

The world's weather is breaking records all the time. As the methods that scientists use to measure the different extremes of weather—from wet and dry to hot and cold to windy and snowy—improve, then even the incredible records described here may one day be broken.

The heaviest hailstone in the world, weighing nearly two and a half pounds, was recorded in Bangladesh in 1986

▲ **Coldest**
*The frozen continent of Antarctica has recorded the coldest temperatures on Earth. The all-time record stands at a staggering 127°F below freezing point. However, extremes such as this are rare. When scientists measured the temperature throughout one whole year, they found that on average it was 72°F below freezing—and even that was a record!*

**Weather balloon**

▲ **Hottest**
*Death Valley in California entered the record books in 1917 as the hottest place on Earth. For 43 consecutive days, temperatures of over 120°F were recorded there.*

Death Valley 120°F

Body heat 98°F

◄ **Windiest**
*Antarctica is not only the coldest place on Earth, but it is also the windiest. At Commonwealth Bay, westerly gales have blown at up to 200 miles per hour.*

**Wind-measuring instrument**

► **Wettest**
The wettest place on Earth is the Shillong Plateau area of India. The rainfall here can be as much as 40 feet each year. Most rain falls between June and September.

**Rainfall-measuring instrument**

Despite the lack of rainfall, plant and animal life can exist even in the world's driest regions

◄ **Driest**
The Atacama Desert in Chile, South America, is the driest place on Earth. It has virtually no rainfall. In some places no rainfall has ever been recorded!

Millions of snowflakes fall in a single snowstorm, all with different six-sided patterns

► **Greatest snowfall**
Snow fall can build up into deep drifts. Over 12 months in 1971–72, more than 100 feet of snow fell on Mount Rainier in Washington State, United States.

# GLOSSARY

**abyssal plain**
A flat area on the seabed covered in a thick layer of mud that stretches for hundreds of miles.

**continent**
A great area of land not broken up by the seas.

**continental slope**
The gently sloping underwater edge of a continent that ends in a steep drop to the ocean's depths.

**delta**
The area at the mouth of a river covered in a silty deposit.

**floodplain**
The area flooded by a river when it breaks its banks.

**geyser**
A natural spring that spouts hot water into the air.

**gorge**
The place at which a river passes along a narrow, steep-sided opening.

**iceberg**
A large piece of floating ice.

**ice sheet**
A dome-shaped glacier that spreads out and covers a large area of land.

**lava**
Molten (liquid) material that comes from deep inside the Earth and oozes out through a volcano.

**pack ice**
A mass of floating ice packed together by winds and currents.

**plate**
Gigantic pieces of land that make up the surface (crust) of the Earth.

**plunge pool**
The pool formed underneath a waterfall, into which the waterfall pours (plunges).

**reef**
A chain or ridge of rocks, sand, or coral at or just above or below the surface of the sea.

**rift**
A deep split or cleft in the surface of the Earth.

**sediment**
The mudlike material that settles at the bottom of the sea.

**solar system**
The sun, the nine planets, and their many moons, together with all the visiting meteors and comets.

**sponge**
A sea animal that has a skeleton that can suck up a large quantity of water.

**taiga**
A Russian term that describes forests that grow in marshy wilderness areas.

**tributary**
A stream or river that flows into another body of water.

---

## MAP INFORMATION

*Information about the geographical features that appear on the map at the front and back of the book can be found in the book itself or listed below.*

## CAVES
**Poll stalactite:**
County Clare, Ireland, 23 feet—longest known free-hanging stalactite in the world

## DESERTS
**Sahara Desert:**
3,320,000 sq mi—largest desert in the world
**Australian Desert:**
600,000 sq mi—2nd largest desert in the world
**Arabian Desert:**
500,000 sq mi—joint 3rd largest desert in the world
**Gobi Desert:**
500,000 sq mi—joint 3rd largest desert in the world

**Patagonian Desert:**
260,000 sq mi: world's 4th largest desert

## LAKES
**Caspian Sea:**
Azerbaijan/Iran/Kazakhstan/Russia/Turkmenistan, Asia, 143,243 sq mi (surface area)—largest lake in the world
**Lake Superior:**
Canada/Michigan/Minnesota/Wisconsin, North America, 31,700 sq mi (surface area)—2nd largest lake in the world
**Lake Victoria:**
Kenya/Tanzania/Uganda, Africa, 26,834 sq mi (surface area)—3rd largest lake in the world
**Lake Huron:**
Canada/Michigan, North America, 23,011 sq mi (surface area)—4th largest lake in the world
**Lake Michigan:**
Illinois/Indiana/Michigan/Wisconsin, North America, 22,317 sq mi (surface area)—5th largest lake in the world

**Lake Titicaca:**
Bolivia/Peru, South America, 12,506 feet—highest navigable lake in the world
**Lake Chad:**
Chad, Africa, 4,000–10,000 sq mi (surface area)—largest lake in West Africa
**Lake Tanganyika:**
Rwanda/Tanzania/Zaire/Zambia, Africa, 13,860 sq mi (surface area)—largest freshwater lake in the world
**Lake Malawi:**
Malawi/Mozambique/Tanzania, Africa, 8,680 sq mi (surface area)—3rd largest of East African Rift Valley lakes

## OCEANS
**Pacific Ocean:**
64,185,714 sq mi (surface area)—largest ocean in the world
**Atlantic Ocean:**
33,420,000 sq mi (surface area)
**Indian Ocean:**
28,350,000 sq mi (surface area)

# INDEX

Page numbers in **bold** refer to illustrations or their captions.

**Arctic Ocean:**
3,662,162 sq mi (surface area)
**Marianas Trench (Pacific Ocean):**
35,827 feet deep—deepest point in the oceans
**Puerto Rico Trench (Atlantic Ocean):**
27,493 feet deep—deepest point in the Atlantic Ocean

## RIVERS

**Yenisey-Angara River:**
Russia, Asia, 3,440 miles—5th longest river in the world
**Ganges River:**
India, Asia, 1,560 miles—world-famous river, which is sacred to the Hindu faith

## VOLCANOES

**Mauna Loa:**
Hawaii, 13,677 feet (30,000 feet from ocean floor)—largest active volcano in the world
**Krakatoa:**
Sunda Strait, between Sumatra and Java, Indonesia, Asia, 2,667 feet—greatest explosion (1883) recorded in history

**Tambora:**
Sumbawa, Indonesia, Asia, 9,255 feet—greatest and most devastating volcanic eruption (1815) in the world ever recorded in history
**Ojos del Salado:**
Chile/Argentina, South America, 22,664 feet—highest active volcano in the world
**Mount St. Helens:**
Washington State, North America, 8,364 feet—erupted in 1980 after being dormant for 123 years
**Surtsey:**
Iceland, Europe, 568 feet—underwater volcanic eruption (1963) that formed the island of Surtsey
**Mount Vesuvius:**
Italy, Europe, 4,190 feet—famous for eruption that destroyed Pompeii in A.D. 79
**Mount Etna:**
Sicily, Europe, 10,902 feet—one of Europe's most active volcanoes, which had a catastrophic eruption in 1669

**Mount Cotopaxi:**
Ecuador, South America, 19,347 feet—one of the world's highest active volcanoes
**Mount Fuji:**
Japan, Asia, 12,388 feet—dormant volcano that is Japan's highest mountain

## WATERFALLS

**Niagara Falls:**
New York State, North America, the two falls are both less than 200 feet tall, but together more than half a mile wide—one of the most famous waterfalls in the world
**Khône Falls:**
Laos, Asia, width=6.7 miles, height=50–70 feet—widest waterfall in the world
**Boyoma Falls:**
Zaire, Africa, flow=600,000 cusec—waterfall with the greatest annual flow in the world
**Victoria Falls:**
Zambia/Zimbabwe, Africa, 355 feet—waterfall discovered by David Livingstone, who named it after Queen Victoria

**NORTH AMERICA**

Mount McKinley
Alaska

Mount Rainier
Washington State

Mount St. Helens
Washington State

Mississippi-Missouri River

Lake Superior
Canada/USA

Lake Michigan
USA

Lake Huron
Canada/USA

Niagara Falls
New York State

Mammoth Cave
Kentucky

Death Valley
California

*PACIFIC
OCEAN*

Mauna Loa
Hawaii

Mauna Kea
Hawaii

Puerto Rico Trench

*ATLANTIC
OCEAN*

Surtsey
Iceland

Poll stalactite
Ireland

Réseau Jean Bernard Cave
France

Cueva de Nerja stalactite
Spain

Mount Cotopaxi
Ecuador

Angel Falls
Venezuela

Amazon River

Lake Titicaca
Bolivia/Peru

**SOUTH
AMERICA**

ATACAMA DESERT

Mount Ojos del Salado
Chile/Argentina

Mount Aconcagua
Argentina

PATAGONIAN DESERT

*WEDDELL
SEA*

*ATLANTIC
OCEAN*

Vinson Massif

South Pole

Polus
Nedostupnosti

*PACIFIC
OCEAN*

Ross Ice Shelf

Lambert Glacier

**ANTARCTICA**

*INDIAN
OCEAN*

Commonwealth
Bay

*WEDDELL SEA*

Vinson Massif
Antarctica